POWER PALS

Adapted by Tracey West from the storyboards by Kevin Kaliher

Based on "THE POWERPUFF GIRLS,"
as created by Craig McCracken

SCHOLASTIC INC.

New York   Toronto   London   Auckland   Sydney
Mexico City   New Delhi   Hong Kong   Buenos Aires

ISBN 0-439-37229-1

Cover and interior illustrations by Mark Marderosian
Cover designed by Peter Koblish/Interior designed by Robin Camera

12 11 10 9 8 7 6 5   3 4 5 6 7/0
Printed in the U.S.A.
First Scholastic printing, May 2002

THE CITY OF TOWNSVILLE!

Where a new day was dawning, and people were sleeping snugly in their beds. Even The Powerpuff Girls were fast asleep.

3

But the Girls' peaceful sleep didn't last long.

BEEP! BEEP!
CLANG! CLANG!
BANG! BANG!

"It can't be garbage day already," said Bubbles in a sleepy voice.

"What's all the **RUCKUS**?" Buttercup wondered.

"Let's go see," Blossom said.

The Girls floated out of bed, rubbed their eyes, and looked out the window.

"Someone is moving in next door," Blossom said.

"Maybe it's someone FUN we can play with," Bubbles guessed.

The Girls flew next door and met
their new neighbor. It was a **LiTTLE
GiRL**! Blossom, Bubbles, and Buttercup
introduced themselves.
"My name is Robin Schneider," said
their new friend.

The Girls liked Robin right away. She liked arts and crafts, just like Bubbles. She liked story time at school, just like Blossom. And she liked playing dodgeball, just like Buttercup.
"Why don't you come over to our house to play?" Bubbles asked her.

"I'D LOVE TO," said Robin. "Who wants to jump rope?"

Blossom, Bubbles, and Buttercup played with Robin all afternoon. "This is the **MOST FUN EVER**!" said Robin.

Then it was time for Robin to go home. The Girls walked her out. But of course, The Powerpuff Girls don't really walk anywhere. They float! Robin was very surprised.

"We forgot to tell you," Blossom said. "We have SUPERPOWERS."

Robin smiled. "Okay," she said. "I have superpowers, too." Robin made her eyes look in two different directions. The Girls giggled.

The next day, the Girls and Robin were having fun on the tire swing when **SUDDENLY** . . .

A signal appeared in the sky! The heart-shaped light meant that the Mayor of Townsville needed The Powerpuff Girls.

"Sorry, Robin," Blossom said. "We have to go and save the day and stuff."

All weekend long, Robin learned that being
friends with superheroes wasn't easy. The
Powerpuff Girls kept having to stop playing
so they could go **SAVE THE DAY**!

POOR ROBIN!
She felt very lonely without her new friends to play with.

Soon it was time for the Girls and Robin to
go to school at Pokey Oaks Kindergarten.

"Sorry we had to keep ditching you to go save the day, Robin,"
Blossom said. "We'll introduce you to all the kids in school."
"IT WILL BE FUN!" Bubbles promised.

But before the Girls could go inside, their teacher
pushed open the door in a **PANIC**.
"Girls! Girls!" cried Ms. Keane. "The Mayor called.
He **NEEDS** you **PRONTO**!"

Blossom sighed. "**SORRY**, Robin," she said. "You'll have to introduce yourself to the class without us. We'll see you later!"

Then The Powerpuff Girls shot up into the sky, leaving Robin all alone.

15

Another little girl watched Blossom, Bubbles, and Buttercup fly away. Her name was Princess Morbucks, and she wanted to be a Powerpuff Girl more than anything in the world. There was one problem: She wasn't a very nice person. Princess was always causing **TROUBLE** for The Powerpuff Girls.

After school, Princess invited Robin
back to her house. They played with
all of Princess's expensive toys while
Princess talked and talked about
herself.

"It's not easy being rich," Princess
chattered on. "There are so many
places to go. So many things to do.
And it's hard keeping up with my
beauty sleep!"

17

"But enough about me," Princess finally said. "Tell me about you — wait! Shut up! The show's about to start."

Robin and Princess watched television on a giant screen. Then a news bulletin interrupted the show.

"We're bringing you the latest **NEWS** about **THE POWERPUFF GIRLS!**" said the newscaster.

"Aw, man," complained Princess. "We're missing our show. Those stupid Powerpuff Girls are always running around, keeping people safe."

SPECIAL · REPORT

"But that's their job," Robin said, defending her friends.

"Yeah, that's what they told me, too," said Princess. "What a line. They just said that because they didn't want to be my friend."

"Really?" asked Robin. She felt so sad. Why had The Powerpuff Girls lied to her?

Princess wasn't telling the truth, of course. But Robin didn't know that. She became really angry with The Powerpuff Girls.

"Don't worry," Princess said. "I have a plan to **GET EVEN** with The Powerpuff Girls!"

Princess told Robin her plan on the way to the Circle J convenience store.

"Okay, Robin," she said. "Now get in there and get what we came for."

"I'm not sure about this," said Robin.

"If you want to get back at those mean Powerpuff Girls, then get going!" Princess snapped.

Robin tiptoed into the Circle J. She took a deep breath. Then she did just what Princess told her to do. She stuffed some candy into her pockets!

CANDY

21

Back in the limo, Princess made a phone call.

"Hello, Mayor," Princess said. "There is a shoplifter at the Circle J. You had better call **THE POWERPUFF GIRLS!**"

Princess hung up the phone. "This is going just as I planned!" she cackled.

Blossom, Bubbles, and Buttercup had no idea what was really happening. They got the Mayor's call and raced to the Circle J to **STOP THE SHOPLIFTER** . . .

23

. . . and instead found Princess in a superhero costume — and Robin all tied up!

"**DON'T WORRY, GIRLS**," Princess said. "I've taken care of everything."

"What's going on?" Blossom asked, shocked.
"I caught this little thief red-handed," Princess bragged.

"Robin, is this true?" Blossom asked.
Robin nodded sadly.
"Well, there you have it," Princess
said. "I guess you'll finally have to let
me be a Powerpuff Girl."

But the Girls knew something
wasn't quite right.

"Let's hear Robin's side of
the story," Blossom said.

"It's true," Robin said. "I
was going to steal the candy.
I was so upset with you for
always leaving me behind to go
save the day."

"That doesn't make it okay to steal," Blossom pointed out.

Princess pointed at Robin. "That's right, you . . . you stealer!" she yelled.

"But stealing candy was your idea," Robin told Princess.

Princess's face turned bright red. "No! You're a liar! And a thief! And I caught you so I deserve to be a Powerpuff Girl!"

27

Blossom, Bubbles, and Buttercup knew Robin was telling the truth. Princess wanted to be a Powerpuff Girl so badly that she had set up the whole thing.

Princess ranted and raved about being a Powerpuff Girl. The sisters just ignored her. They took Robin by the hand and left the Circle J.

"We're sorry we left you behind all the time," Buttercup said.

SLAM!

"It was never because we didn't like you," Blossom added.
"It's just our job," Bubbles explained.
"I know," Robin said.

Back home, the Girls and Robin were playing on the swings
when the hotline rang. Professor Utonium answered it.
"Professor, get the Girls. IT'S AN EMERGENCY!" the
Mayor yelled. "My pickle jar's stuck and I'm starving!"

"The Girls are pretty busy right now, Mayor," said the Professor. "Maybe they could come by later." That was just fine with The Powerpuff Girls. They knew saving the day was important. But so was spending time with their **FRIEND**!

31

So once again the day — and friendship — was
saved, thanks to **THE POWERPUFF GIRLS!**